Date: 11/26/14

**J BIO CARVER
Aliki.
A weed is a flower : the life of
George Washington Carver /**

A Weed is a Flower

The Life of George Washington Carver

Written and illustrated by **ALIKI**

Simon & Schuster Books for Young Readers

An imprint of Simon & Schuster
Children's Publishing Division
1230 Avenue of the Americas
New York, NY 10020
Also Availbale in a paperback edition from Aladdin Paperbacks

Manufactured in China

10 9 8

Library of Congress Cataloging-in-Publication Data.
Aliki.
   A weed is a flower: the life of George Washington
Carver / written and illustrated by Aliki.
   Summary: Text and pictures present the life of the
man, born a slave, who became a scientist and devoted
his entire life to helping the South improve its
agriculture.
   1. Carver, George Washington, 1864?–1943—Juvenile
literature. 2. Agriculturists—United States—
Biography—Juvenile literature. [1. Carver, George
Washington, 1864?–1943. 2. Agriculturists. 3. Afro-
Americans—Biography.]   I. Title.
S417.C3A65 1988   630'.92'—dc19
[B]   [92]   87-22864

ISBN 978-0-671-66118-2 (hc)
ISBN 978-0-671-66490-9 (pbk.)
0813 SCP

for Lisa, Jim, Stephen and Gregory Liacouras

When George Washington Carver was born,
he had many things against him. He was a sick,
weak, little baby. His father had just died,
and his mother was left alone to care for him
and for his brother, James.
And even worse, he was the son of slaves.
There was no hope for the future.

But George Washington Carver was no ordinary man.
He was a man who turned evil into good,
despair into hope and hatred into love.
He was a man who devoted his whole life to helping
his people and the world around him.

This is his story.

George Washington Carver was born in Missouri
in 1860—more than a hundred years ago.
It was a terrible time.
Mean men rode silently in the night,
kidnapping slaves from their owners
and harming those who tried to stop them.

One night, a band of these men rode up to the farm
of Moses Carver, who owned George and his mother, Mary.
Everyone ran in fear. But before Mary could hide her baby,
the men came and snatched them both,
and rode away into the night.

Moses Carver sent a man to look
for them. Mary was never found.
But in a few days, the man returned
with a small bundle wrapped in his coat
and tied to the back of his saddle.
It was the baby, George.

Moses and his wife, Susan, cared for Mary's children.
George remained small and weak. But as he grew,
they saw he was an unusual child.
He wanted to know about everything around him.
He asked about the rain, the flowers, and the insects.
He asked questions the Carvers couldn't answer.

When he was very young, George kept a garden
where he spent hours each day caring for his plants.
If they weren't growing well, he found out why.
Soon they were healthy and blooming.
In winter he covered his plants to protect them.
In spring he planted new seeds.
George looked after each plant as though
it was the only one in his garden.

Neighbors began to ask George's advice
about their plants, and soon he was known
as the Plant Doctor.

As time went on, George wondered
about more and more things.
He wanted to learn and yearned
to go to school.

In the meantime, the slaves had
been freed, but schools nearby
were not open to blacks.
So when he was ten,
George left his brother, his garden,
and the Carver farm and went off
to find the answers to his questions.

Wherever George Washington Carver found schools,
he stayed. He worked for people to earn his keep.
He scrubbed their floors, washed their clothes,
and baked their bread. Whatever George did,
he did well. Even the smallest chore
was important to him.

Some people took George in as their son.
First he stayed with Mariah and Andy Watkins, who
were like parents to him. Then he moved to Kansas
and lived with "Aunt" Lucy and "Uncle" Seymour.
They, too, loved this quiet boy who
was so willing to help.

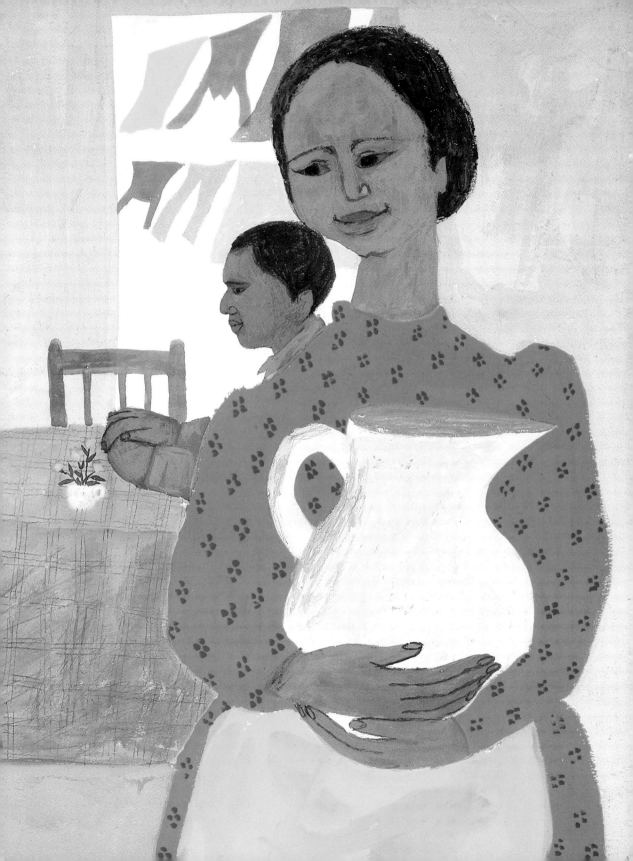

George worked hard for many years,
always trying to save enough money for college.
Other boys, who had parents to help them,
were able to enter college much sooner than George.
He was thirty before he had saved enough.
Still, it was not that simple.
Not all colleges would admit blacks,
even if they had the money to pay.

George was not discouraged. He moved to Iowa,
and found a college which was glad to have
a black student.

At college, George continued to work. He opened
a laundry where he washed his schoolmates' clothes.

And, he continued to learn. His teachers and friends
soon realized that this earnest young man
was bursting with talents. He played the piano,
he sang beautifully, and he was an outstanding painter.
In fact, for a time he thought of becoming an artist.

But the more George thought of what he wanted to do,
the more he wanted to help his people.
And he remembered that his neighbors used to call him
the Plant Doctor.

He had never forgotten his love for plants.
In all the years he had wandered, he always
had something growing in his room.

So, George Washington Carver chose to study
agriculture. He learned about plants, flowers, and soil.
He learned the names of the weeds. Even they were
important to him. He often said: a weed is a flower
growing in the wrong place.

He still asked questions. If no person or book
could answer them, he found the answers himself.
He experimented with his own plants,
and found secrets no one else knew.

When George finished college, he began to teach.
He was asked to go to Alabama, where a college
for blacks needed his talent. It was there,
at Tuskegee Institute, that George Washington Carver
made his life.

In Alabama, Professor Carver taught his students
and the poor black farmers, who earned
their livelihood from the soil. He taught them
how to make their crops grow better.

Most of the farmers raised cotton. But sometimes
the crops were destroyed by rain or insects,
and the farmers couldn't earn enough to eat.

Professor Carver told them to plant other things
as well. Sweet potatoes and peanuts were good crops.
They were easy to grow. He said that raising only cotton
harmed the soil. It was better if different crops
were planted each year.

The farmers did not want to listen. They were afraid
to plant peanuts and sweet potatoes. They were sure
that no one would buy them.

But Professor Carver had experimented in his
laboratory. He had found that many things
could be made from the sweet potato. He made soap,
coffee, and starch. He made more than a hundred things
from the sweet potato.

And even though people in those days called
peanuts "monkey food," Professor Carver said they
were good for people, too. Besides, he found
that still more things could be made from the peanut.
Paper, ink, shaving cream, sauces, linoleum, shampoo,
and even milk! In fact, he made three hundred different
products from the peanut.

Once, when important guests were expected at
Tuskegee, Dr. Carver chose the menu. The guests
sat around the table and enjoyed a meal of soup,
creamed mock chicken, bread, salad, coffee, candy,
cake, and ice cream. Imagine their surprise
when they learned that the meal was made
entirely from peanuts!

Slowly, the farmers listened to George Washington Carver. They planted peanuts and sweet potatoes. Before they knew it these became two of the most important crops in Alabama.

Soon the whole country knew about Dr. Carver
and the great things he was doing. He was honored
by Presidents and other important people. Every day,
his mailbox bulged with letters from farmers
and scientists who wanted his advice. He was offered
great sums of money, which he turned down.
Money was not important to him. He did not even bother
to cash many of the checks he received.

Throughout his life, George Washington Carver
asked nothing of others. He sought only to help.
He lived alone and tended to his own needs.
He washed his clothes and patched them, too.
He used the soap he made and ate the food he grew.

Dr. Carver was asked to speak in many parts
of the world, but he did not leave Tuskegee often.
He had things to do. He continued to paint.
He worked in his greenhouse and in his laboratory,
where he discovered many things. He discovered
that dyes could be made from plants, and colors
from the Alabama clay. Even when he was over
eighty and close to death, Dr. Carver kept working.
Night after night, while the rest of the town
lay asleep, a light still shone in his window.

The baby born with no hope for the future
grew into one of the great scientists of his country.
George Washington Carver, with his goodness
and devotion, helped not only his own people, but all peoples
of the world.